For my parents,
who always encourage me to follow my dreams,
no matter what they are —A.L.

ISBN 978-0-06-236412-8

The artist used Adobe Photoshop to create the digital illustrations for this book.
Typography by Joe Merkel
16 17 18 19 20 SCP 10 9 8 7 6 5 4 3 2 1
❖
First Edition

CHICKEN in SPACE

By Adam Lehrhaupt
Illustrated by Shahar Kober

HARPER
An Imprint of HarperCollinsPublishers

Zoey wasn't like the other chickens.

She had dreams.

She had a plan.

She had a pig.

"Put your hat on, Sam," said Zoey.
"We're going to space!"
    "Before lunch?" asked Sam.
"Before pie? Is that a good idea?"
    But Zoey was already off.

"Henry," said Zoey, "come to space with us."
"No, thanks," said Henry. "I've got space right here."
"Not open space," said Zoey. "Outer space!"

"Pip," said Zoey, "come to space with us."
"Sounds dangerous," said Pip.
"Not dangerous," said Zoey. "An adventure!"

"Clara," said Zoey, "come to space with us."
"You don't have a ship," said Clara. "You can't
go to space without a ship."

"Not a problem!" said Zoey. "An opportunity!"

"Zoey always finds a way," said Sam.
"Look, Sam! I found a ship!" said Zoey.
"Of course you did," said Sam.

SPACE!

"Wow," said Zoey.
"Space is beautiful."

"So is pie," said Sam.
"See any pie?"

Zoey looked.

"Watch out for the ball!" said Sam.

"Not a ball!" shouted Zoey.
"An ASTEROID!"

"Watch out for the kite!"
said Sam.

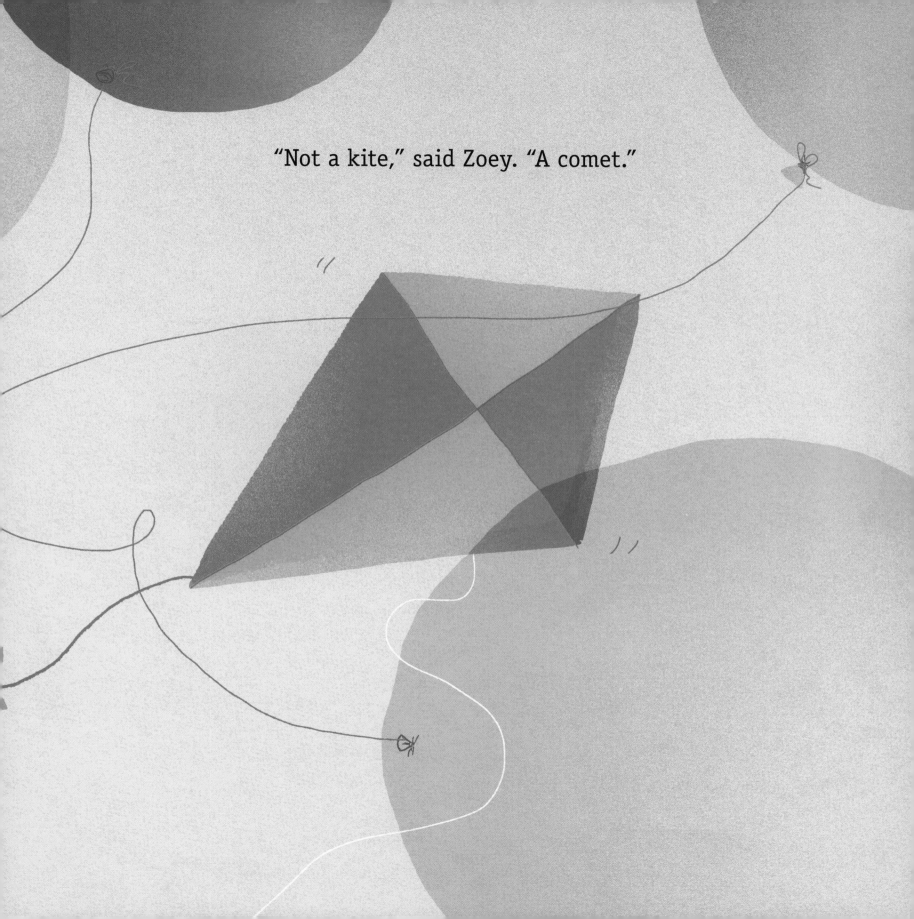

"Not a kite," said Zoey. "A comet."

POP!

"Watch out for the birds!" said Sam.
"Not birds," said Zoey. "Alien attack ships."

"We're going down!" yelled Sam.
"Prepare for landing!" said Zoey.

"Perfect!" said Zoey. "Zoey to ground control. I repeat, Zoey to ground control. We made a perfect landing."

"Perfect?" asked Sam. "There isn't any pie!"

Back at the barn, the animals gathered to hear about Zoey and Sam's big adventure.

"We went to space," said Sam. "We were hit by an asteroid. We dodged a comet. And we battled aliens." Everyone was impressed.

"How did you do it?" asked Clara.
"Zoey always finds a way," said Sam.
"I just wish we'd found some pie."

Zoey tapped Sam's shoulder.

"For me?" asked Sam. "Is it pie?"

"Not just a pie," said Zoey.
"A moon pie!"

Sam broke off a piece of his pie for Zoey...

but she was already planning their next adventure.